# I wish I could... SLEEP!

## A story about being brave

Tiziana Bendall-Brunello

Illustrated by John Bendall-Brunello

QED Publishing

Little Bear was trying to go to sleep when he heard a strange screeching sound.

Little Bear felt a bit scared.

"Oooooh!" he said to himself. "I wonder what that was?"

Little Bear peered round the edge of the cave.

"Hello, Little Bear!" said Owl. "What are you doing out here?"

"Well, I heard a scary sound coming from the tree..." replied Little Bear.

"That was only ME!" said Owl.

"I wish I could sleep,"
yawned Little Bear.

"Why don't you try my bed?" suggested Owl.

Without another thought Little Bear climbed into Owl's nest.

He tried to make himself comfortable.

He wriggled a bit.

He turned a bit.

But just then...

# CRACK!

And Little Bear started to fall.

"Ooohhhh!"
called Little Bear.

Luckily Little Bear fell right into a big pile of leaves.
"Now I really do want to go home to MY bed,"
he sighed.

But he was suddenly startled by something rustling in the leaves beside him.

"Ooooooh!" Little Bear froze.

"Hello, Little Bear!" said Raccoon. "What are you doing here?"

"Ahh, it's you," said Little Bear. "I just want to go back to my bed. I wish I could sleep."

"I need to collect more leaves to make my bed warm and cosy," said Raccoon. "But you can try sleeping in my bed."

But try as he might, Little Bear could only just get his nose down the hole.

"Oooh, I just want to go home," wailed Little Bear.

So off he went... but just then he saw a
strange shadow moving slowly across the path.
"Oooooh!" cried Little Bear. "What's that? It looks like a..."

"Hello, Little Bear!" said Moose gently. "Don't be afraid. It's only me. What are you doing out here?"

"I couldn't sleep, but now I just want to go back to my bed," said Little Bear.

"Jump up here then – I'll give you a ride!" said Moose.

"Now try to think of happy things to help you go to sleep. That's what I do!"

In no time at all, Little Bear
was fast asleep.